A Thousand NO's

written by

DJ CORCHIN

illustrated by

DAN DOUGHERTY

sourcebooks
eXplore

She had a great idea.

Or at least she thought she did.

That's when she got her first NO.

It was heavy.
It was hard to carry.
And it kinda hurt.

It's just one NO, she thought.
Surely I can handle ONE NO.

Then she got a second NO.

UGH!

This NO was heavier than the last.

And it was harder to carry.

And it hurt even more.

She tried to stop them,
but the NO's got inside her idea.

Her idea got bigger.

Enough, she thought.

Then...

ANOTHER NO!

And another NO!

AND
ANOTHER!

Not only did her idea get heavier,
but it got poked and twisted,
and it started to change shape.

Her idea got so big.
It was clear she needed help.

She wasn't sure how she felt about someone else helping with her idea.

After all, it was HER idea.

But this called for drastic measures.

REALLY drastic measures.

NO after NO after NO came.
Some of them made her
idea challenging.

Some of them made it easier.

Some split it into pieces.

There were just so many NO's.
She needed more and
more people to help.

But soon, something
interesting happened.

She began to get curious about what her idea might end up looking like. In fact, it became fun for everyone to add more NO's and see how her idea would change and grow.

NO 997, NO 998, NO 999...

And on the thousandth NO,
she looked up and saw her great idea.

"That's a lot of NO's."

It didn't look anything like it did before.

But she was ok with that.

To Tracy, Duke, Audrey, and Elliot

Published by Sourcebooks eXplore, an imprint of Sourcebooks Kids
P.O. Box 4410, Naperville, Illinois 60567-4410
(630) 961-3900
sourcebookskids.com

Originally published in 2016 in the United States of America by The phazelFOZ Company, LLC.

Library of Congress Cataloging-in-Publication Data is on file with the publisher.

Source of Production: PrintPlus Limited, Shenzhen, Guangdong Province, China
Date of Production: June 2020
Run Number: 5019078

Printed and bound in China.
PP 10 9 8 7 6 5 4 3 2

Also, the author is perfectly at ease with his use of apostrophes in this book.